EPISODE 1. THE HAUNTED HOUSE

Table of Contents

Chapter 1. Taken

October 10th, 2014

A massive hurricane was going through Louisiana.

A ship had gone missing in the storm

Zoe Baker

On October 10th, 2014; there was a massive hurricane that tore through Louisiana. During that time, a ship went missing and flooding was prominent. Zoe Baker helped her family as her father Jack, former U.S Marine, rescued a young girl from the storm. He took her in alongside another woman he rescued, as his wife Marguerite and son Lucas helped. Getting the girl a fresh change of clothes, the girl suddenly snapped awake and told Zoe she was taken over as the lights suddenly cut out. She soon found Lucas knocked out, and her mother was suddenly possessed, spouting that the girl had given her a gift as insects erupt out of her mouth. In a panic, Jack held her back as he urged Zoe to get some rope. But by the time she returned, Jack now acted bizarrely, mutilating himself to show his devotion to the girl, Eveline. In a panic, Zoe got away as Jack snatched Lucas and forced him to accept Eveline's gift.

Zoe's father, Jack rescued a young girl from the storm

Jack rescued a young girl from the storm (2)

Jack told Zoe to take care of the rescued girl.

Jack Baker

Jack would go to check on the boathouse.

The little girl was still unconscious.

Suddenly, she woke up.

The little girl told Zoe that she had been taken and the light went out all of sudden.

Feeling scared, Zoe quickly went searching for the other members of her family.

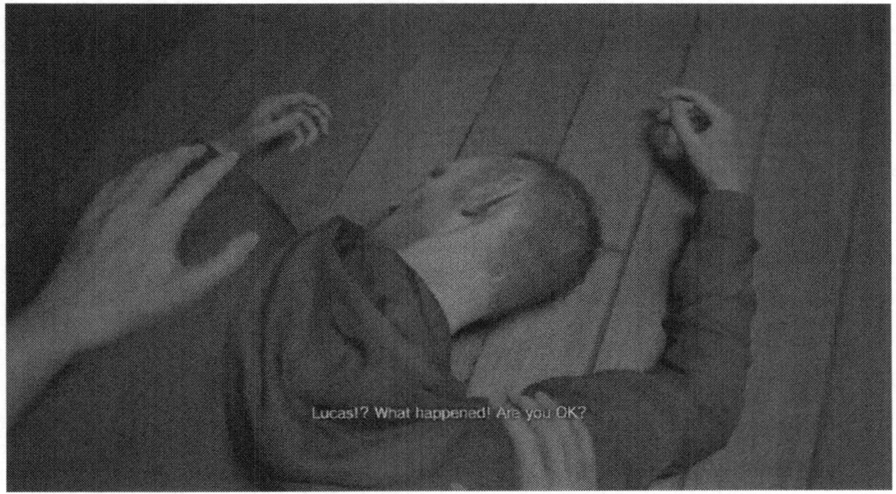

Lucas Baker, Zoe's brother was knocked out.

Marguerite, Zoe's mother

Marguerite was possessed

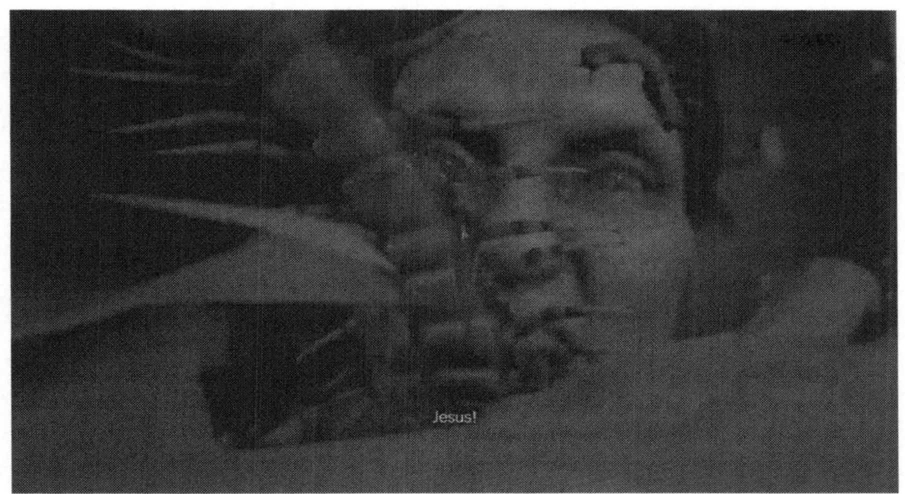

Insects were coming from her mouth

Jack pushed her back and urged Zoe to get some ropes.

Jack pushed her back and urged Zoe to get some ropes (2)

By the time Zoe came back, her father was possessed, too.

Zack was talking and acting very strangly

He stabbed himself to show devotion for the young girl he had rescued.

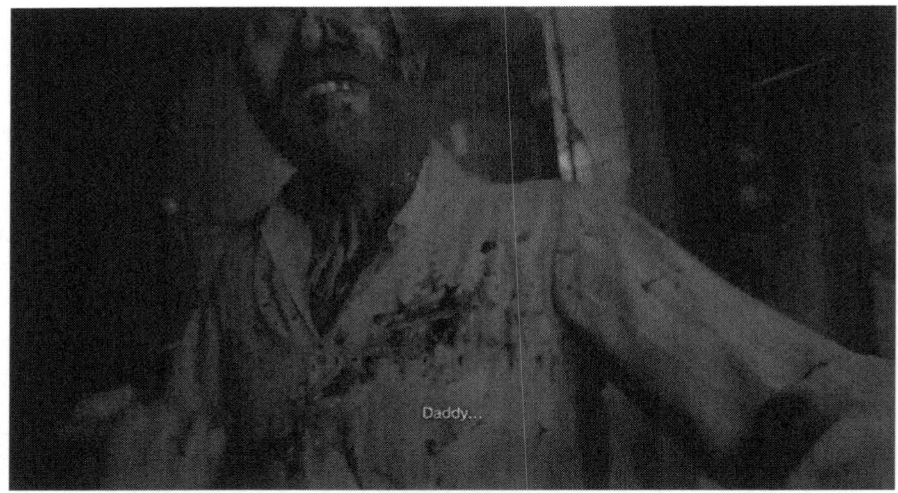

Jack also caught Lucas and forced him to accept 'Eveline's gift'.

It turned out that the name of the rescued girl was Evaline.

Jack forced Lucas to accept 'Eveline's gift' (2)

Jack forced Lucas to accept 'Eveline's gift' (3)

On the way to escape, Zoe found the other woman that Jack had rescued and her notes also. The note said that if they found an abandoned girl, please avoid her at all costs.

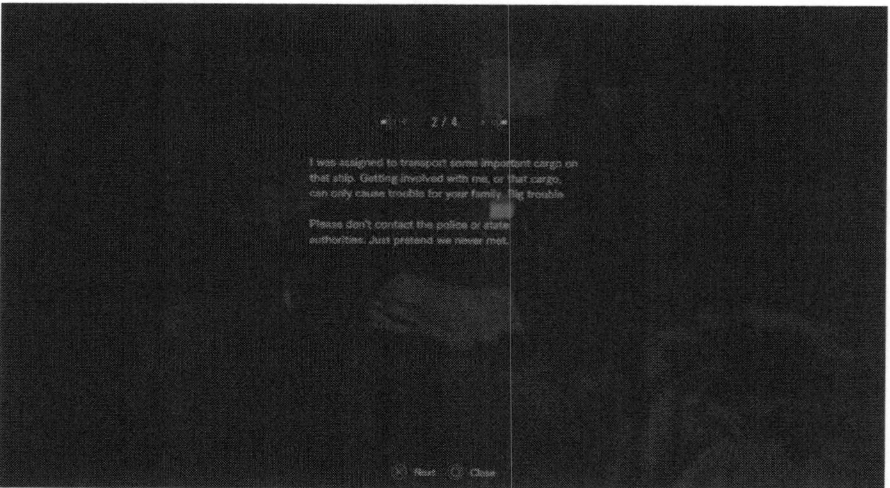

The woman's note (1)

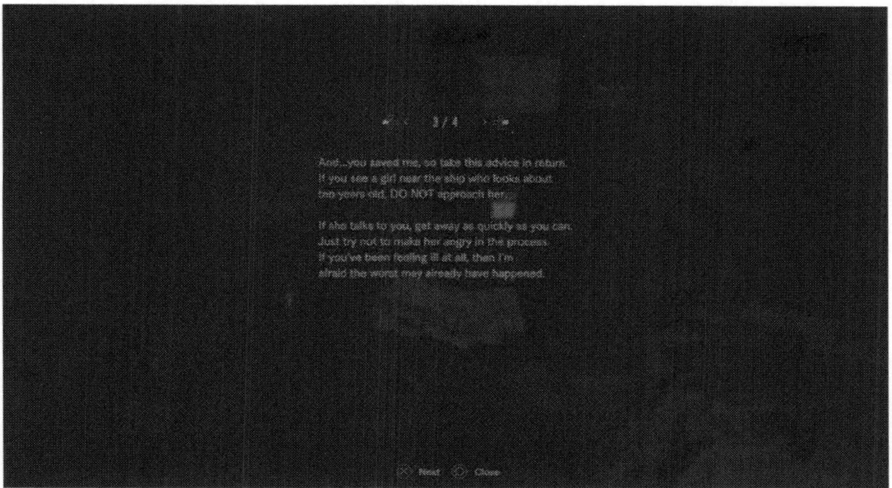

The woman's note (2)

The woman's note (3)

It might be too late for them now. But the note said that there might be a kind of Serum out there that could cure her family's current condition.

Unexpectedly, Evaline caught up to Zoe.

A scary smile ...

Everything went dark after that ...

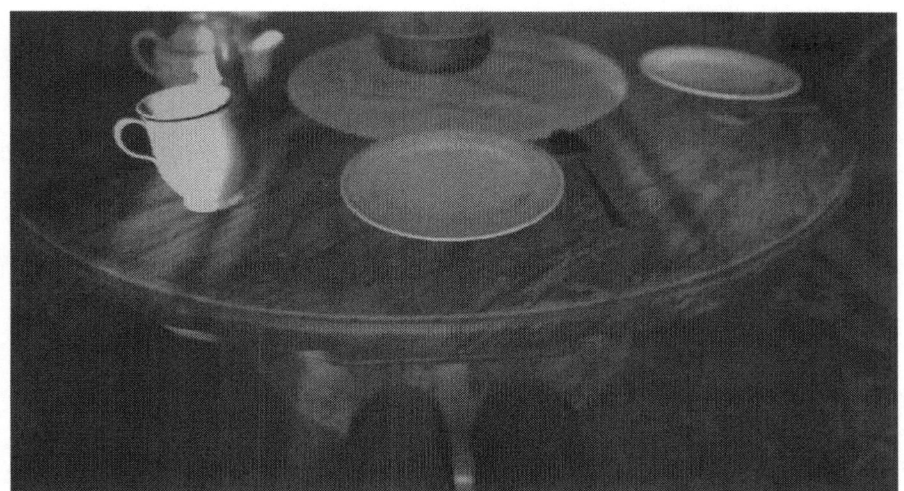

The next day ...

Everything seemed normal again ...

Zack said he had had a bad dream about a little girl ...

But was that really a dream?

Retreating to her trailer, Zoe found the other rescued woman there, who left them a note explaining she had been assigned to transport particular cargo on the ship; and if they saw a little girl near the ship, they should avoid her at all costs. If they began feeling odd, she warned them it was likely already too late, but there was a serum that could cure them. However, Eveline was already upon her. The next day, things seem normal as it nothing had happened, buts its clear the family was now under the control of Eveline, and only Zoe could do something about it and her now-insane family. 3 years passed, and in 2017, a man named Ethan suddenly received a distress message from his wife Mia who had been missing for 3 years, and found again in Dulvey, Louisiana. Driving up to a mysterious plantation house called the Baker Farm, he spotted an odd abandoned van for the web show Sewer Gators that checked out rumored ghost houses.

While everything last night seemed so real ...

Was that really a dream?

In a magical way, Zoe seemed infected & resisted 'Evaline's gift' !
I wonder why Zoe remained uninfected after her family was all taken?
The plot armor vaccine, I mean her will power must be very strong

Chapter 2. The Haunted House

3 years after ...

It was 2017

A man named Ethan received a message from his long-lost wife, Mia.

She said she was in Dulvey, Louisiana.

His wife had been lost for 3 years.

A Planatation house named Baker Farm

An abandoned van

This van was from the web show ‘Sewer Gators’ checking out rumored ghost houses.

He spotted clues confirming Mia was somewhere here, and entered the strangely quiet home. Investigating, he found a hidden passageway into the basement where clearly not all was well, and a list of names had been all but Mia and a man named Clancy were either dead or turned. He soon found Mia locked in a cell, and freeing her, she seemed confused and panicked, insisting she didn't send him a message. Attempting to escape now, Mia suddenly turned crazed and stabbed at the defenseless Ethan, and for a moment, she returned to normal, claiming someone was possessing her. Turning insane again, Ethan was forced to defend himself, lodging an axe into Mia, and as he now attempted to escape himself, a phone suddenly rang nearby. Picking it up, it was Zoe on the other end as she warned and informed him there was a way out through the attic. Finding a videotape and watching it, he saw that it was from Clancy and it had been made in June earlier in the year.

Ethan spotted some evidences that claimed Mia was here. He decided to investigate the 'ghost house'

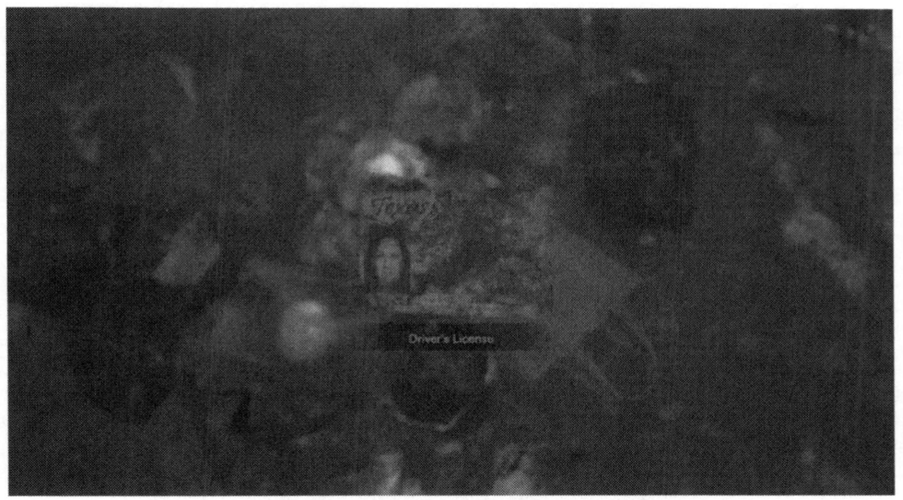

Investigating the ghost house

A mysterious van was from the web show ‘Sewer Gators’ checking out rumored ghost houses.
Wait! Wait! Wait! Is ghost real?
No. Ghosts are not real. But zombies are real!

Investigating the ghost house (2)

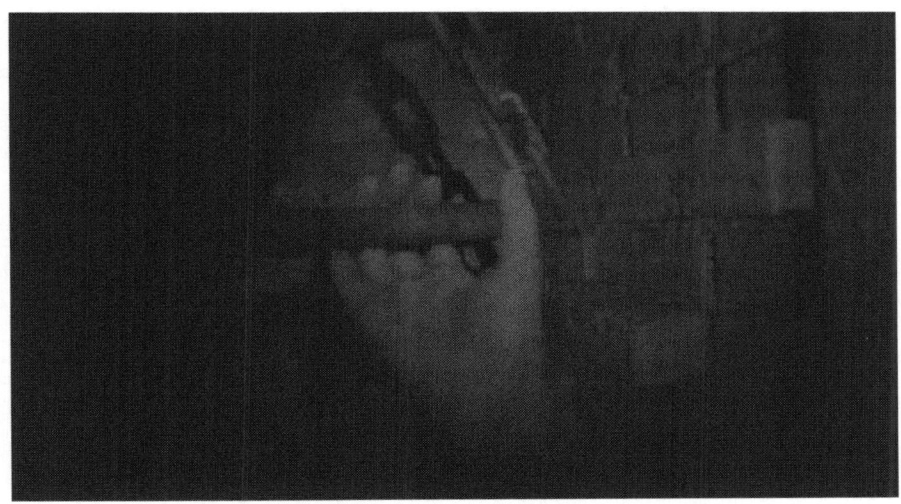

Investigating the ghost house (3)

Investigating the ghost house (4)

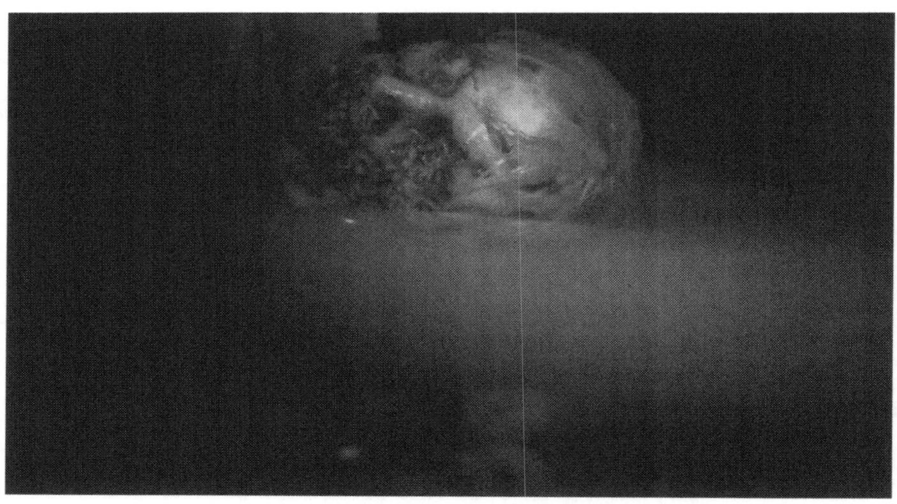

Investigating the ghost house (5)

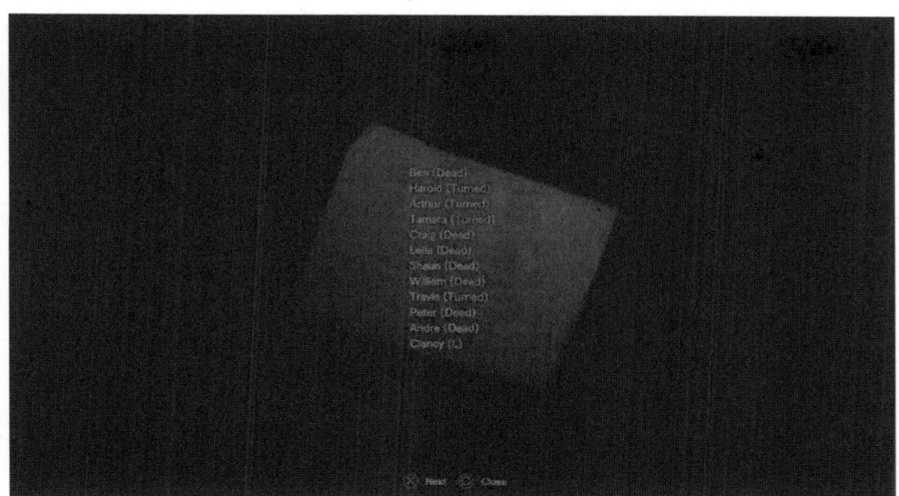

A list of names was found

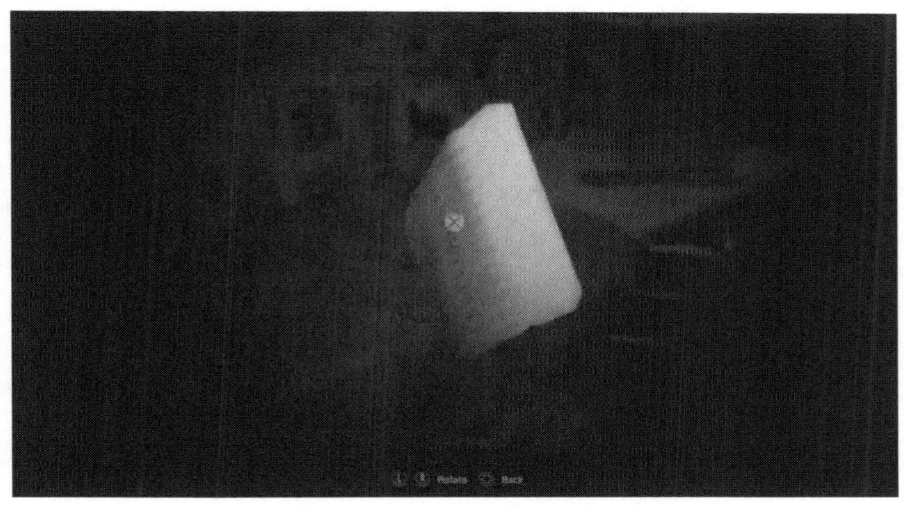

Mia's name was on the list

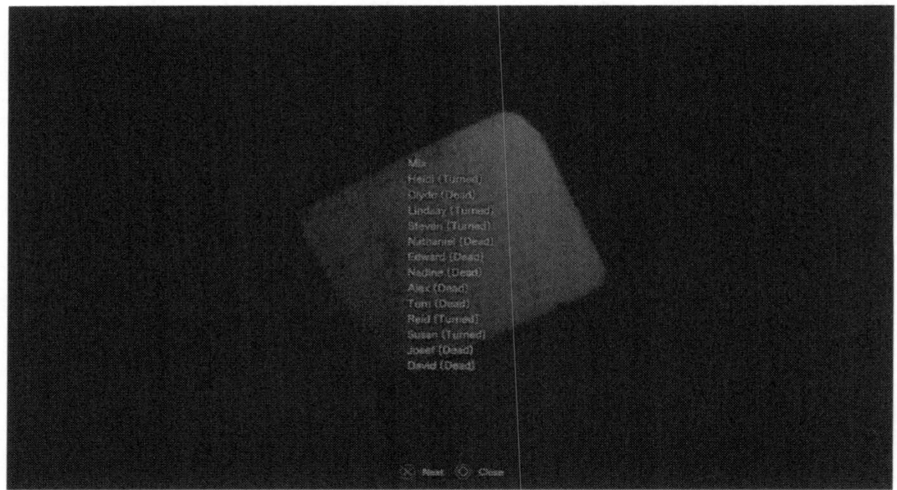

Investigating the ghost house (6)

Mia was found.

Mia was locked in a cell.

Mia insisted that she hadn't been the one who sent Ethan the message.

Rescuing Mia

Rescuing Mia (2)

Mia suddenly became possessed and attacked Ethan.

Mia became possessed and attacked Ethan (2)

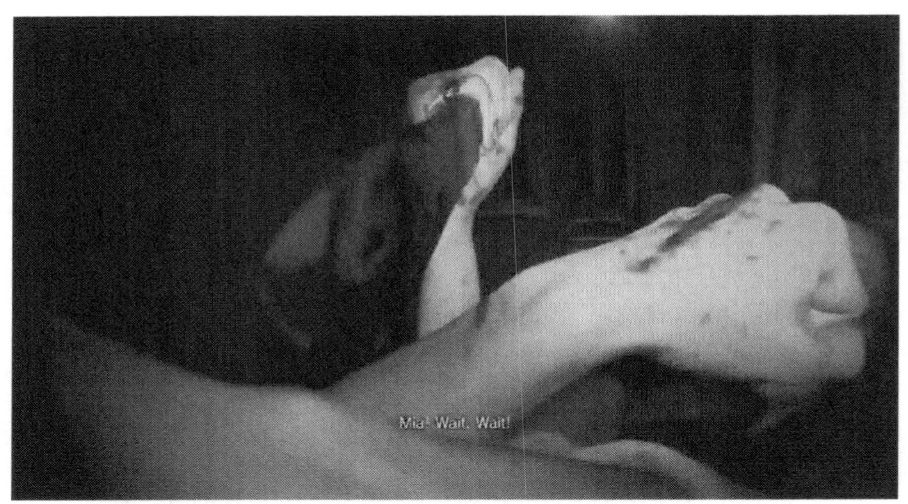

Mia became possessed and attacked Ethan (3)

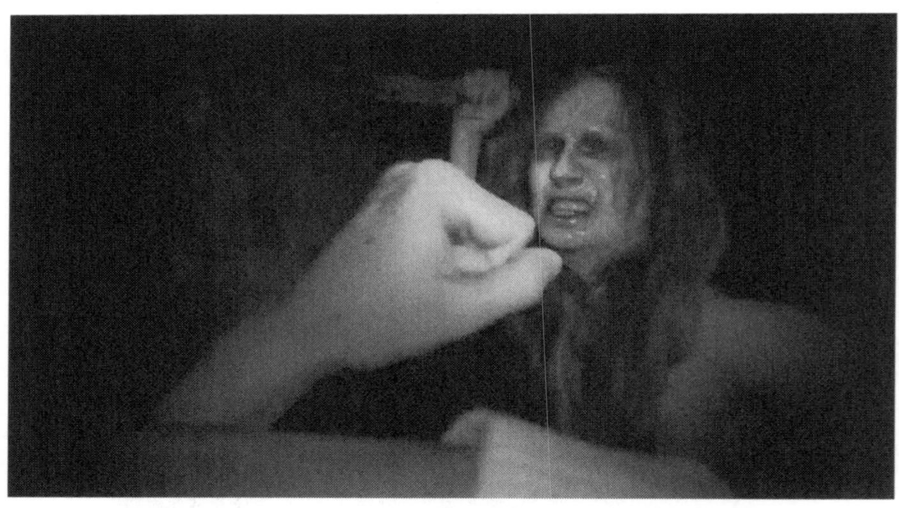

Mia became possessed and attacked Ethan (4)

Mia became normal.

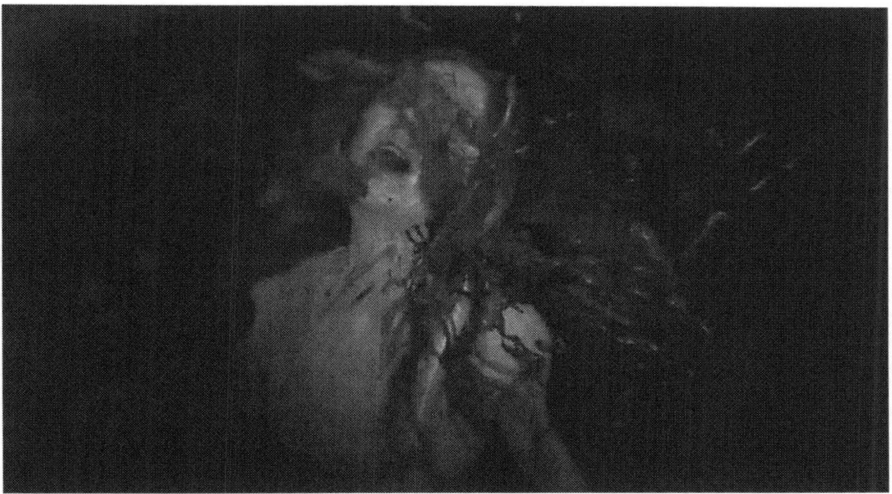

She became insane again and Ethan had to defend himself.

Ethan ran away from his wife.

A telephone rang.

It was Zoe.

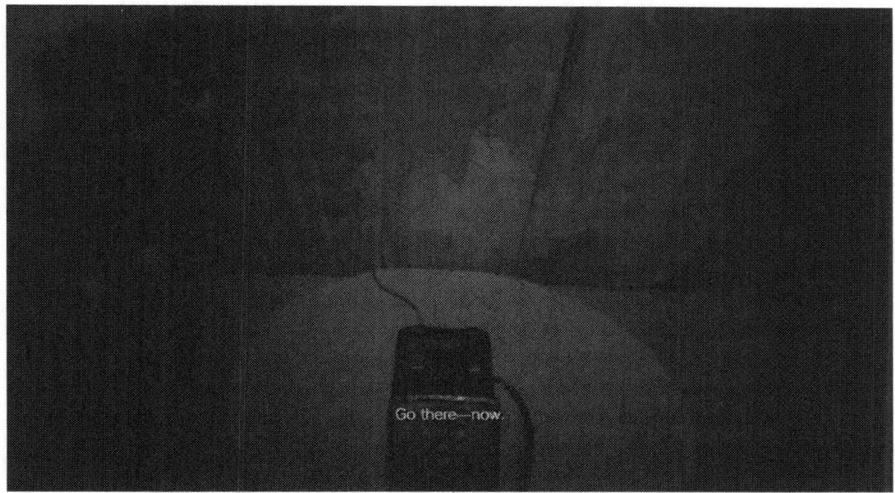

Zoe instructed Ethan a way to get out of the house.

Ethan received a call from Zoe guiding him a way out of the ghost house.

Wait! Wait! After 3 years, she hasn't gone insane? While living with a family like that?

Why didn't she just run away and find a cure? She must have accepted Evaline as her sister

Dulvey Haunted House Footage from Clancy Javis

Dulvey Haunted House Footage from Clancy Javis (2)

Why must he watch that video footage at that time? When his life was in danger? He could take that video footage and watch it later
GALAXY

Dulvey Haunted House Footage from Clancy Javis (3)

Dulvey Haunted House Footage from Clancy Javis (4)

Dulvey Haunted House Footage from Clancy Javis (5)

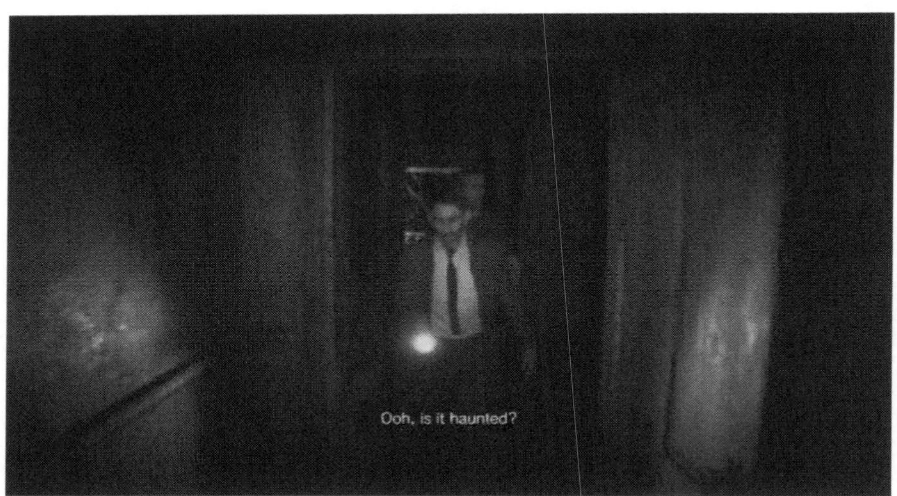

Dulvey Haunted House Footage from Clancy Javis (6)

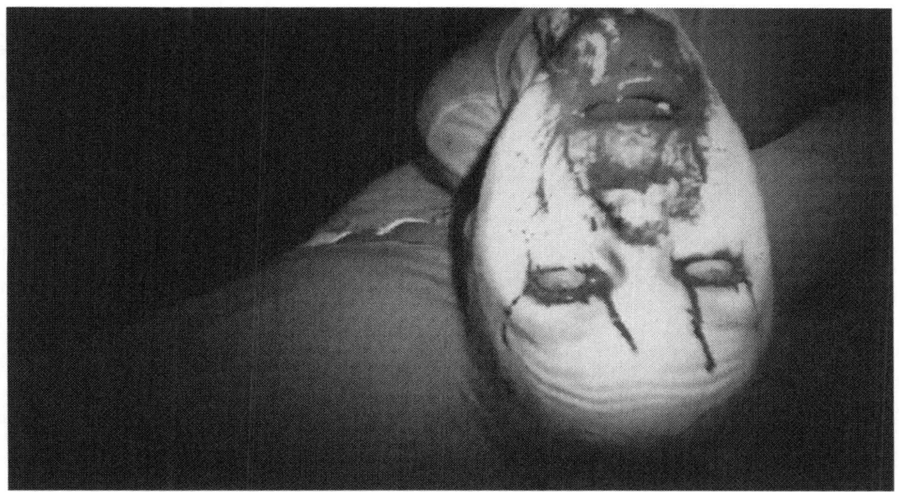

Mia continued attacking Ethan.

Mia continued attacking Ethan (2)

Mia continued attacking Ethan (3)

Mia continued attacking Ethan (4)

Ethan fought back.

Ethan fought back (2)

Jack knocked Ethan unconscious.

Jack knocked Ethan unconscious (2)

In that tape, Clancy had been the cameraman for the Sewer Gators show in which the crew had been rehearsing for an episode in this supposedly abandoned house, though they met a foul end by the hands of someone else lurking in the dark. With supernatural strength and regeneration, Mia again assaulted him, pinning him to the wall with a screwdriver and using a chainsaw to cut off his hand. Finding a gun, he was forced to put her down again. After that, a strange man grabbed him and knocked him out, welcoming him to the family. Fading in and out of consciousness, he observed his hand get reattached by Zoe, and woke up at a dinner table, before Jack, his wife Marguerite, their son Lucas and an emaciated old woman in a wheelchair. Ethan's resistance to their meals offended them before a doorbell ringing distracted them away, allowing Ethan a window to break free.

Ethan was welcomed to the 'family'

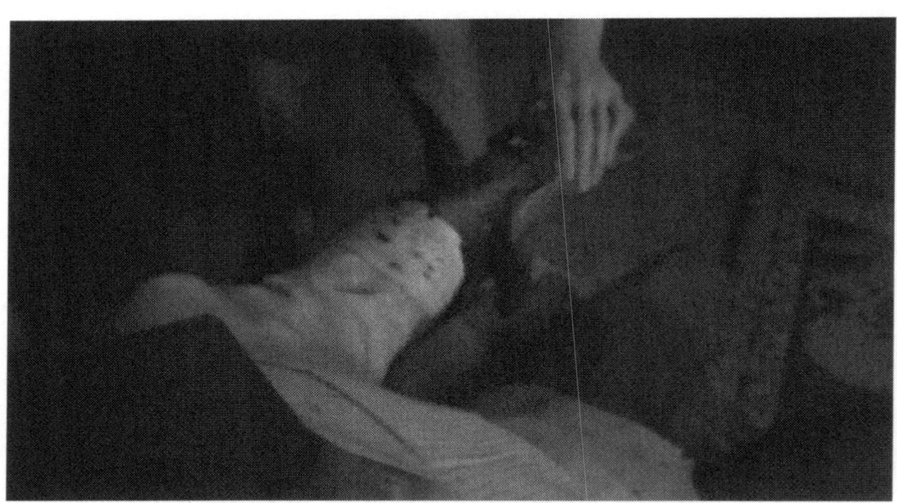

Ethan was welcomed to the 'family' (2)

Ethan was welcomed to the 'family' (3)

Ethan was welcomed to the 'family' (4)

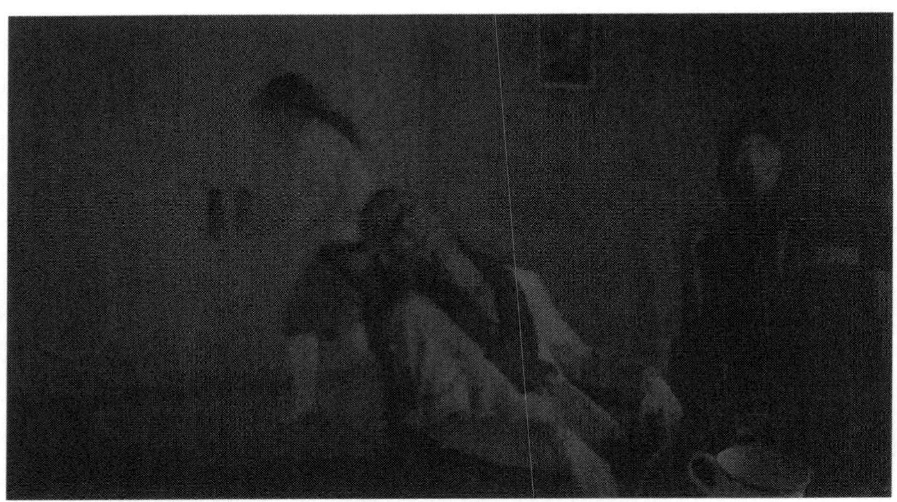

Ethan was welcomed to the 'family' (5)

Ethan was welcomed to the 'family' (6)

Ethan was welcomed to the 'family' (7)

Ethan broke free

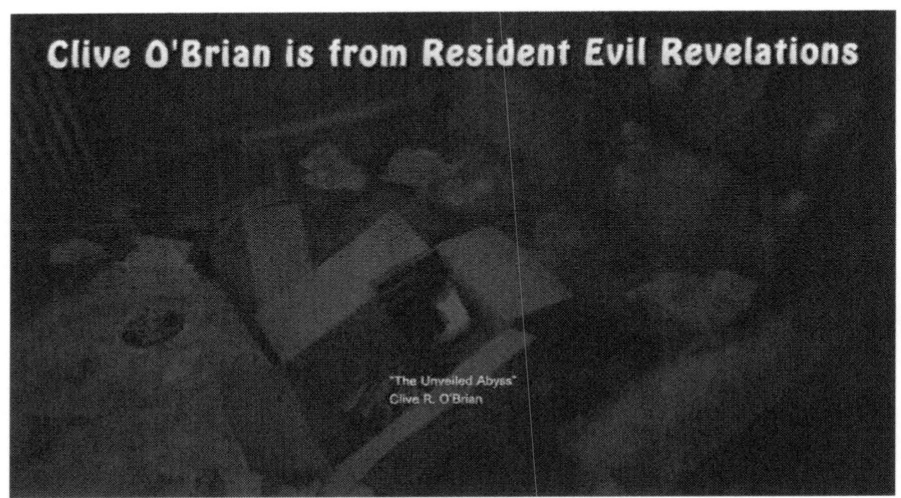

A Book named 'the Unveiled Abyss'

Ethan spotted a deputy

Did he really have to read that 'Resident Evil: Revelation' Book at that time? He could take it home and read it later on on his sofa.
GALAXY

The garage

The garage (2)

Passing by a revealing book from a familiar author, he spotted the visitor who happened to be a deputy investigating several missing people in this area. Meeting him in the garage, they barely had a chance to speak, before Jack sneaked up behind the deputy and stabbed him through the head with a shovel. Getting inside the car, Ethan tried to run over Jack but Jack somehow kept getting back up, and even boasted of how unkillable he was with a direct headshot. Reading an article from a familiar outbreak reporter, he also read a note about a bad storm in the past that washed up a large ship in the bayou. Finding another videotape, this time from Mia in July, Ethan saw her account of fleeing from Marguerite within the house, seeing a strange little girl, and failing to escape the terror. Jack now interrupted his attempted to flee, showing off remarkable regeneration, and strange new monsters now formed from the pitch black mold colonies littered around the house.

Zack attacked the deputy.

The deputy was killed.

Fighting Jack for a way out

Fighting Jack (2)

Fighting Jack (3)

Fighting Jack (4)

Fighting Jack (5)

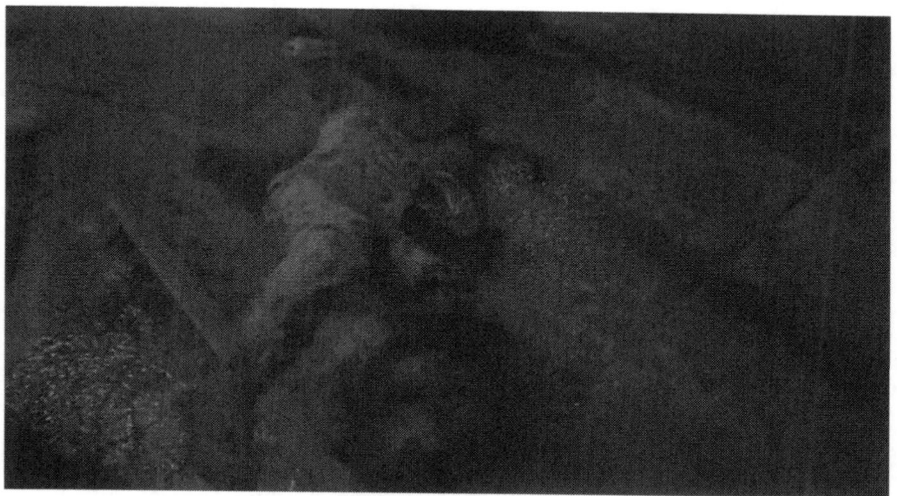

Fighting Jack (6)

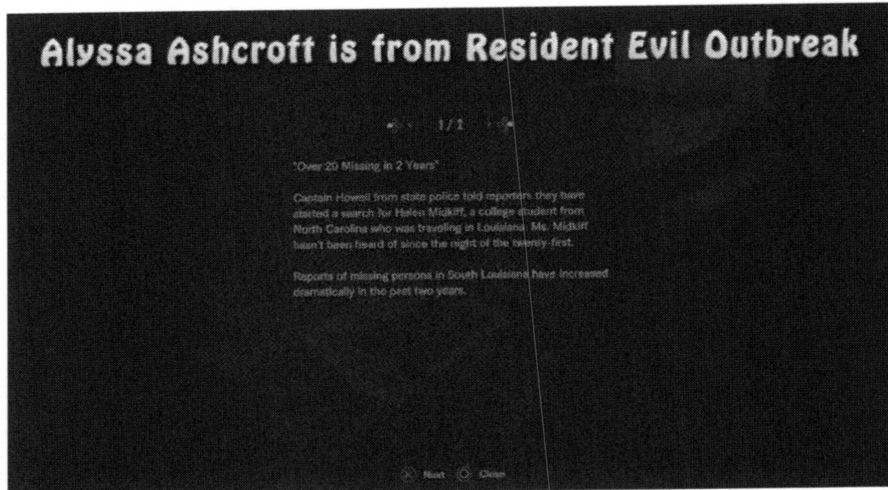

An article from an disaster reporter

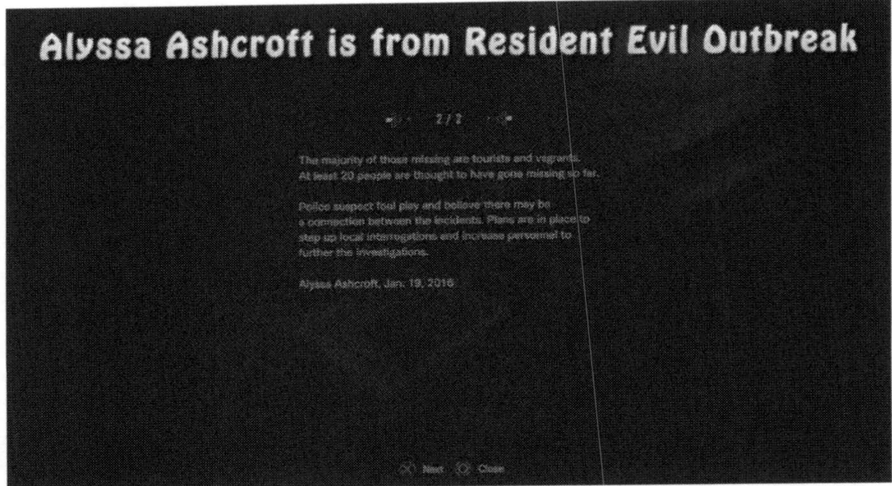

An article from an disaster reporter (2)

He could use his phone to take picture of that article and read it later!
GALAXY

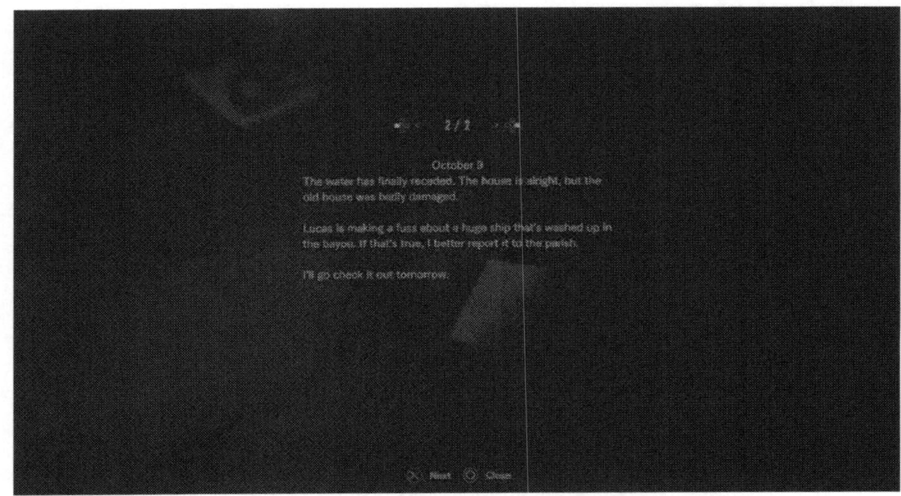

An article from an disaster reporter (3)

Ethan found another videotape and watched it

This video was about Mia's failed escape attempt

This video was about Mia's failed escape attempt (2)

Fighting Jack again

Fighting Jack again (2)

Fighting Jack again (3)

Fighting Jack again (4)

Fighting Jack again (5)

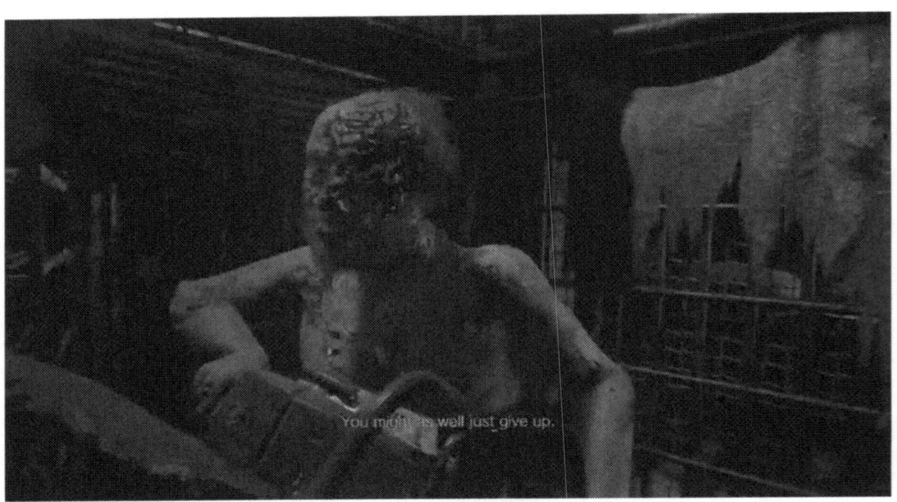

Fighting Jack again (6)

Fighting Jack again (7)

Fighting Jack again (8)

With no choice but to confront Jack, Ethan dueled him for the key to freedom, and ripped and tore past Jack's abnormal regeneration to edge out a win. Finding Zoe's trailer, he heard from Zoe that she, her family, and Mia were all contaminated, and they have no hope of leaving until they could be cleansed of it. There was a serum that could cure them as long they weren't too far gone, but she didn't know where it was, but thought her mother hid it in the old house part of the property. Finding the old house waterlogged, deserted and infested with insects courtesy of Marguerite, Ethan found a flamethrower and used it to burn his way through, soon finding Mia again, though before they could talk for long, Lucas snatched her away. In pursuit, he found noted on synthesizing a serum cure, involving parts from specimens of something called D-Series and the help of Zoe.

Chapter 3. The Serum

Jack was defeated.

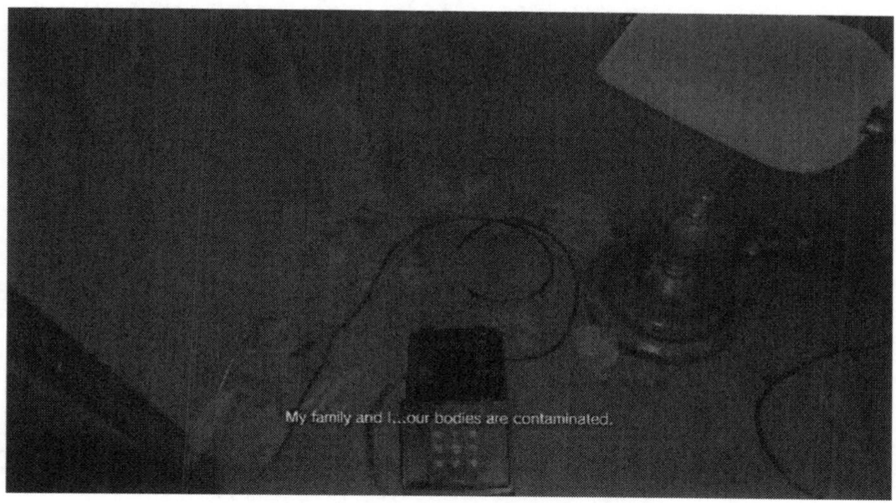

A message recorded by Zoe

A message recorded by Zoe (2)

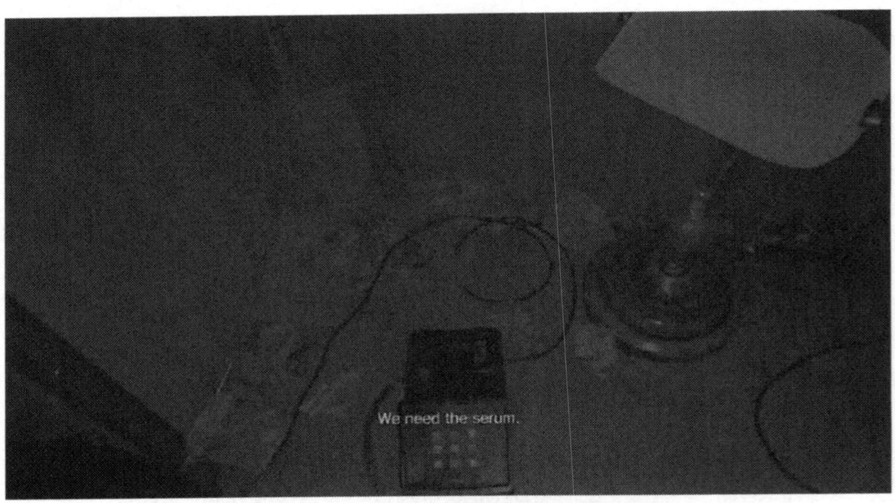

A message recorded by Zoe (3)

A message recorded by Zoe (4)

A message recorded by Zoe (5)

A message recorded by Zoe (6)

Exploring the old warehouse

Exploring the old warehouse (2)

Exploring the old warehouse (3)

Exploring the old warehouse (4)

Ethan found Mia again. This time, she seemed normal.

But she was taken away by Lucas soon.

D-Series mystery

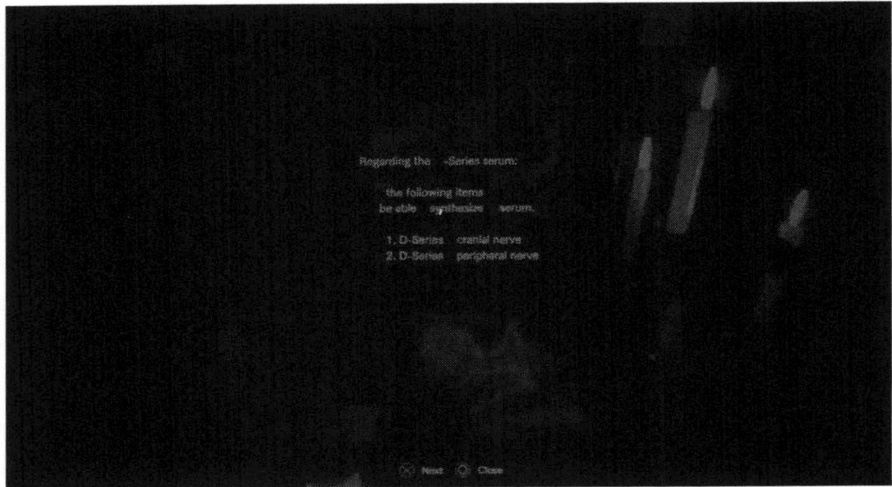

D-Series mystery (2)

D-Series mystery (3)

He clashed with Marguerite, who had mutated into a powerful, grotesque insectile form, and after she was defeated, she calcified and crumbles immediately. When retrieving a part needed for the serum, he again spotted a strange little girl eluding him. After trying to meet up with Zoe to make a cure, Lucas made the announcement that he was captured Zoe as well, and wanted to have a little fun with Ethan. Leaving a disturbing trail of clues for Ethan to find, he still ran into the odd old woman in even odder locations. He found Lucas' room, and learnt he was quite good with machines and traps, and even the house had been renovated by a familiar contract company which explained the odd passageways and locked doors. He also found a cassette tape showing the fate of Clancy. After being captured by Jack, he had been bounded in a kitchen with his coworker.

Fighting Marguerite

Fighting Marguerite (2)

Fighting Marguerite (3)

Retrieving a part of the serum

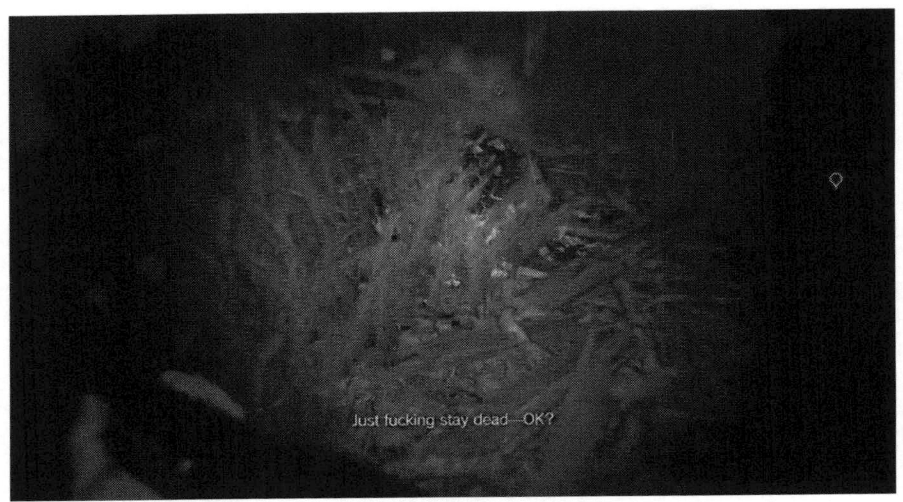

Retrieving a part of the serum (2)

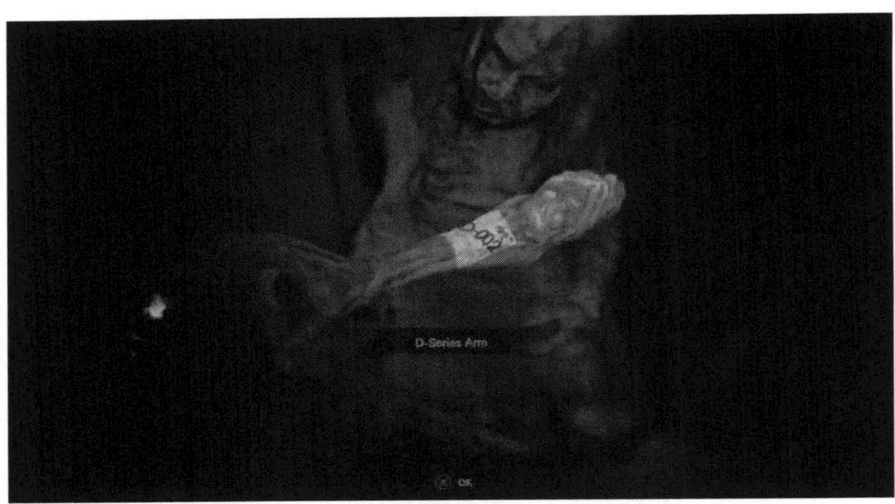

Retrieving a part of the serum (3)

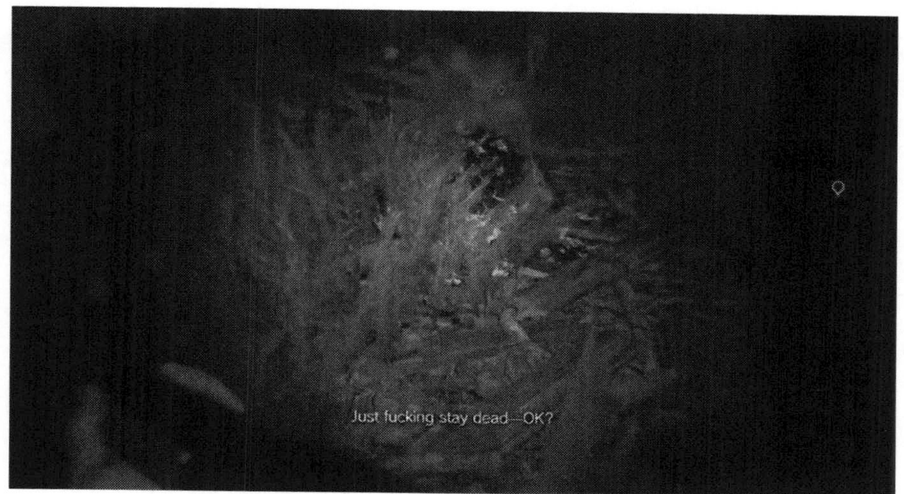

Retrieving a part of the serum (4)

Getting back to Zoe to make a cure

Lucas said that he had taken Zoe as well.

Lucas had kept both Zoe and Mia.

Lucas had kept both Zoe and Mia (2)

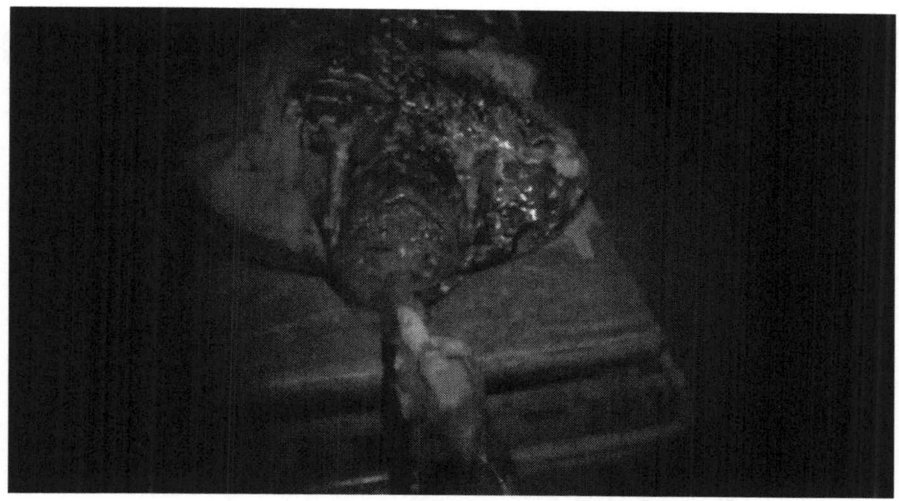

Finding Zoe and Mia

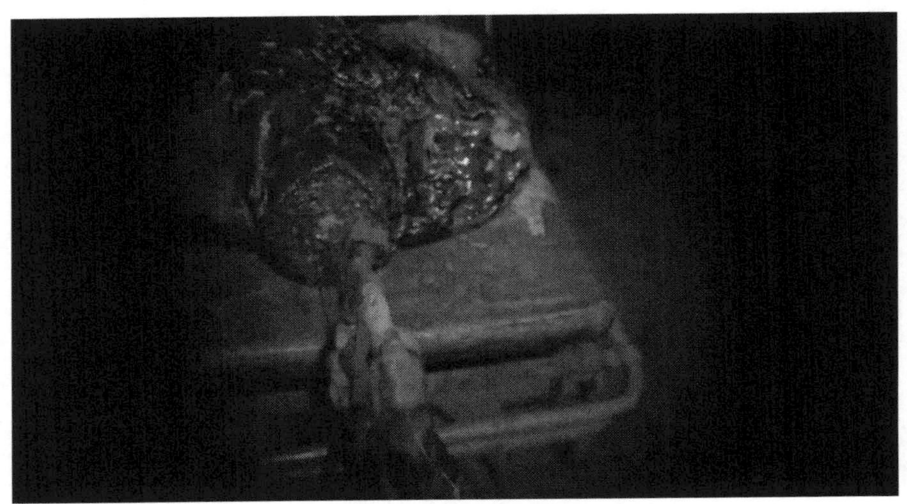

Finding Zoe and Mia

Lucas' Room

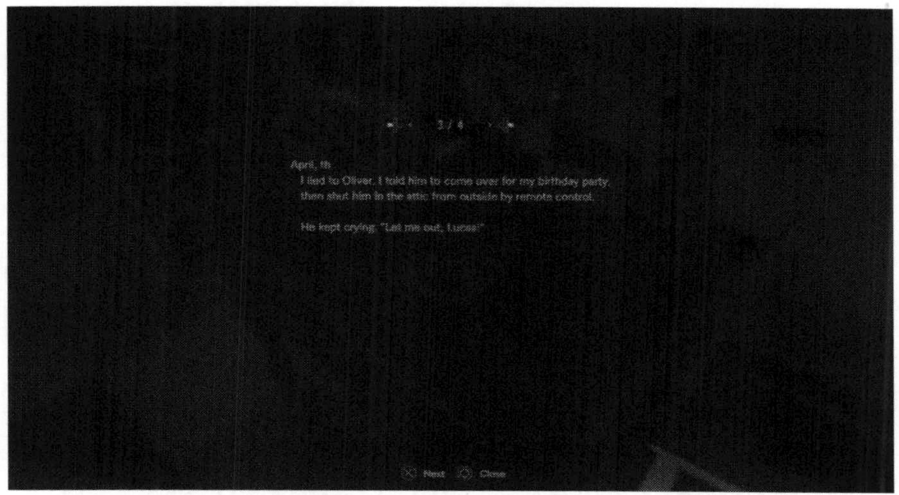

A cassette tape revealing the fate of Clancy

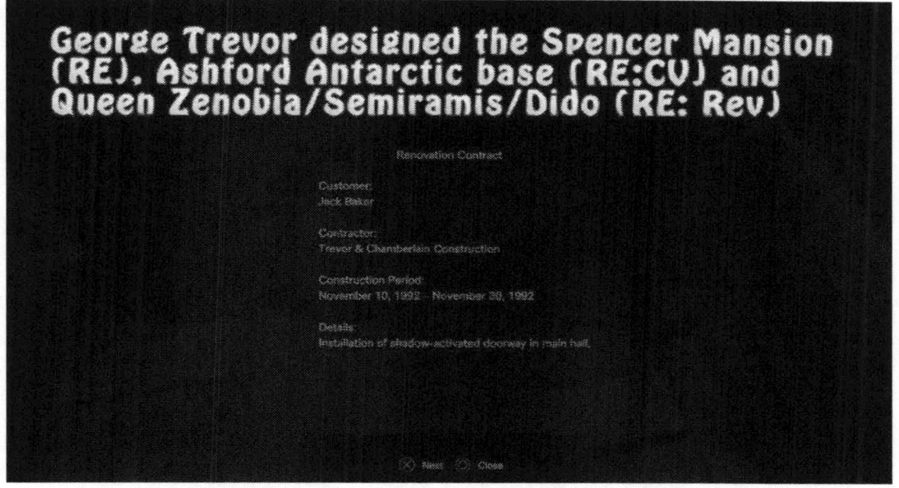

A cassette tape revealing the fate of Clancy (2)

A tape revealing the fate of Clancy (3)

A tape revealing the fate of Clancy (4)

Ethan watched the tape showing Clancy's Fate.

Wait! Why didn't Lucas attack Ethan while he was busy watching the footage?

Lucas must be a gentleman with good manner. He would attack once Ethan finished watching that.

A tape revealing the fate of Clancy (5)

A tape revealing the fate of Clancy (6)

A tape revealing the fate of Clancy (7)

A tape revealing the fate of Clancy (8)

A tape revealing the fate of Clancy (9)

A tape revealing the fate of Clancy (10)

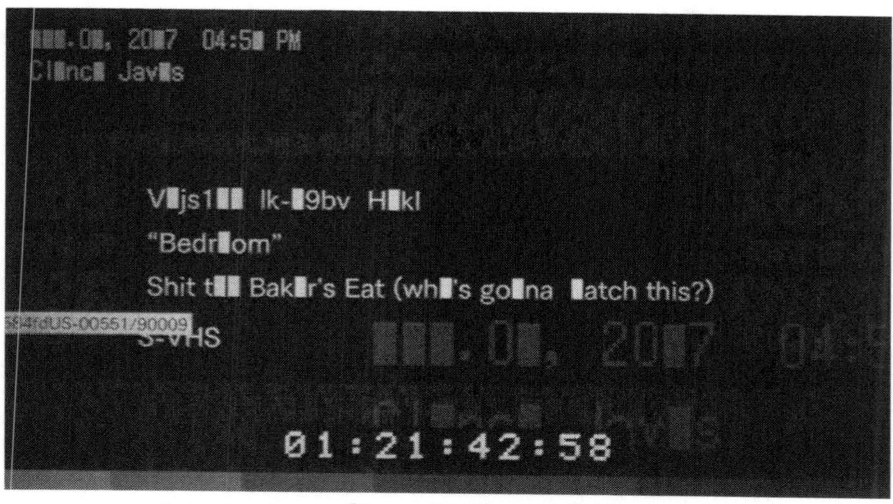

A tape revealing the fate of Clancy (11)

A tape revealing the fate of Clancy (12)

A tape revealing the fate of Clancy (13)

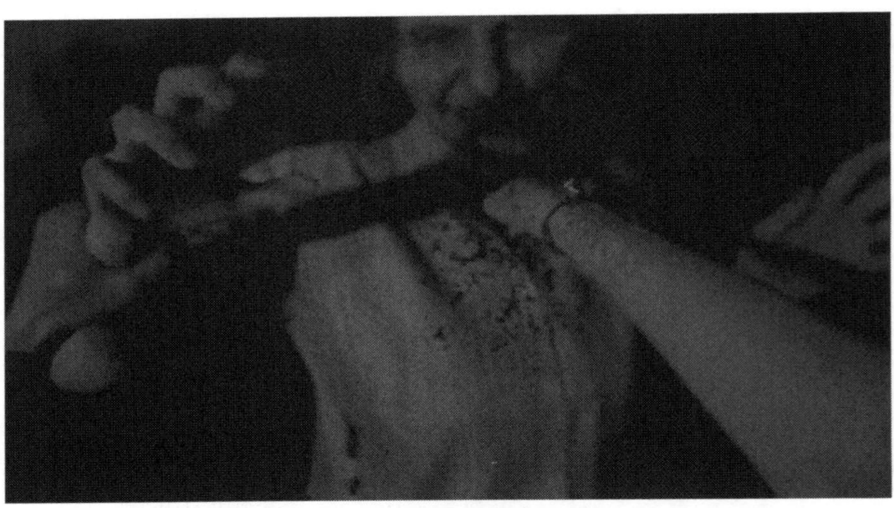

A tape revealing the fate of Clancy (14)

Though his coworker struggled to get him free, he had been murdered and decapitated by an insane Mia. After failing to escape, Jack threw him in a basement with growing waves of Molded to attack him, and again Clancy barely survived the night. Afterwards, he had been bound again and made to be turned by Marguerite, playing along and solving the puzzles to open a trap door until he stabbed her in the neck and to flee through a trap door. Unfortunately, it led to Lucas who captured him and forced him to test his luck in a deadly game of blackjack. Clancy won, much to Lucas's frustration, and as a result, Clancy had been locked in a puzzle room, though unfortunately, solving it had been an explosive trap that lead to Clancy's own immolation and demise. Lucas sent Ethan another warning that he knows Zoe was helping him make a serum, but he wouldn't allow it.

A tape revealing the fate of Clancy (13)

A tape revealing the fate of Clancy (14)

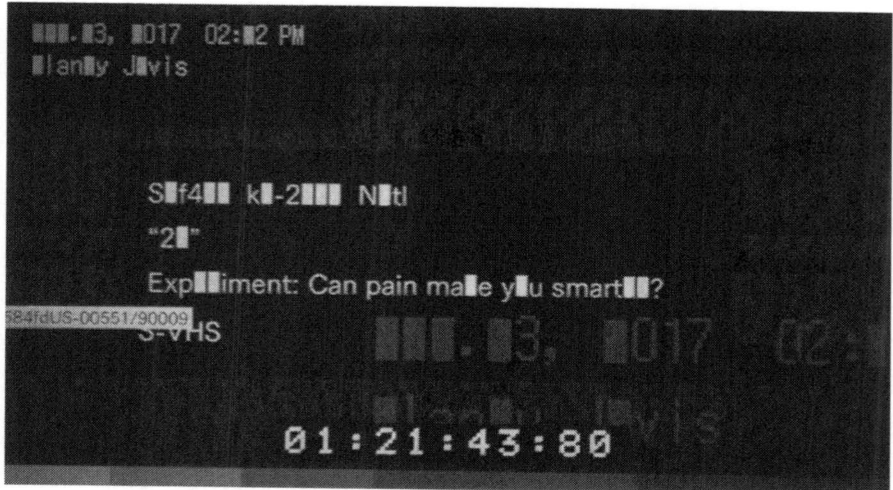

A tape revealing the fate of Clancy (13)

A tape revealing the fate of Clancy (14)

A tape revealing the fate of Clancy (15)

A tape revealing the fate of Clancy (16)

A tape revealing the fate of Clancy (17)

A tape revealing the fate of Clancy (18)

Unfortunately, Clancy died painfully in vain.

Unfortunately, Clancy died painfully in vain (2)

Lucas sent Ethan another warning

Lucas sent Ethan another warning (2)

Not even the safe rooms were safe as booby-traps litter the path to Lucas, as Ethan passed the remains of Clancy, and Lucas locked Ethan into the same trap room that killed Clancy. However, thanked to the clues gained by the unfortunate Clancy, Ethan was able to sidestep the deathtrap and overcome it, and chased Lucas away, gaining the other element of the serum cure. Beyond, he found Mia and freed her, and finally came face to face with Zoe. She took the ingredients from Ethan and quickly manufactures two serums, but Ethan quickly took them as a colossal mutated Jack crashed through the pier. Ethan put down Jack but Jack refused to stay down. At Zoe's command, Ethan jammed one of the serums into Jack, and it worked instantly, halting the molded transformation, calcifying and disintegrating him for good. However, with only one serum left, Ethan was left with the hard choice to cure either Zoe or Mia.

Lucas locked Ethan into the same trap room that killed Clancy.

Lucas locked Ethan into the same trap room that killed Clancy (2)

Lucas locks Ethan into the same trap room that killed Clancy.

I bet Ethan would survive

Yeah. Poor Clancy didn't have the plot armor and ability to respawn.

Lucas locked Ethan into the same trap room that killed Clancy (3)

Lucas locked Ethan into the same trap room that killed Clancy (4)

Chapter 4. A Hard Choice

Ethan escaped.

Ethan got another element for the Serum.

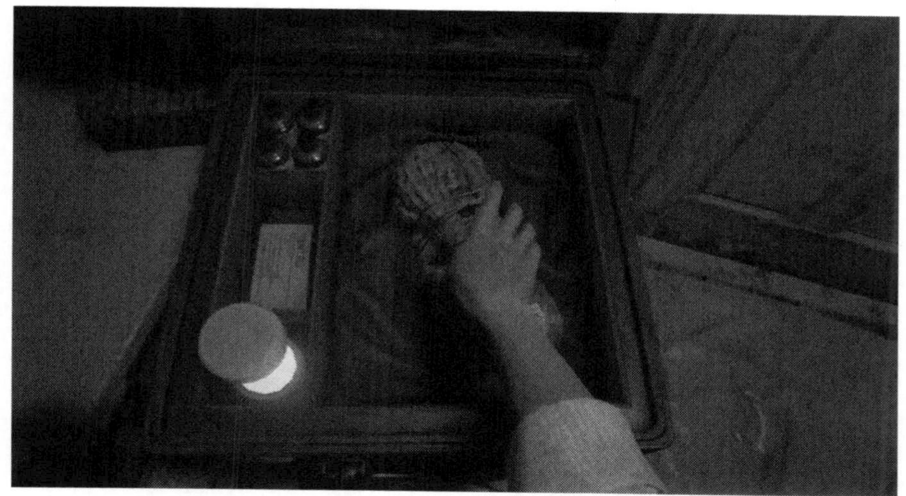

Ethan got another element for the Serum (2)

Mia was found.

Finally, Ethan met Zoe.

Ethan quickly gave Zoe all the gathered ingredients.

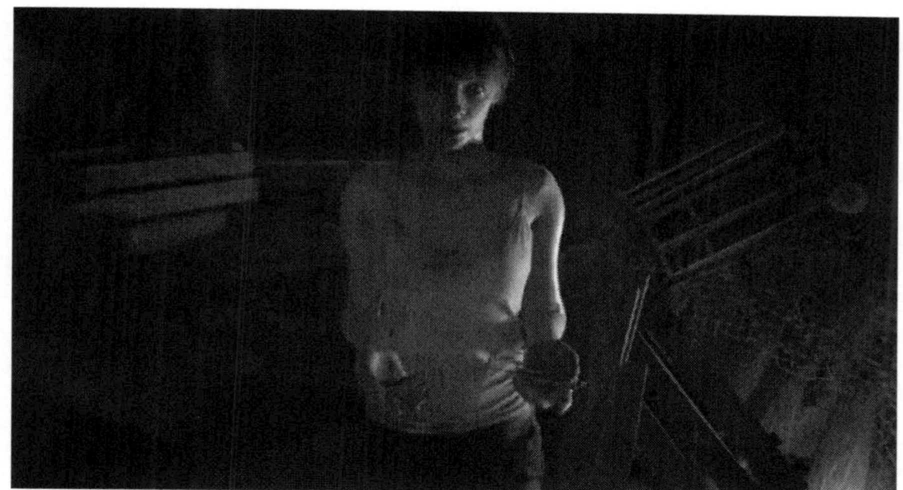
Zoe made 2 serums.

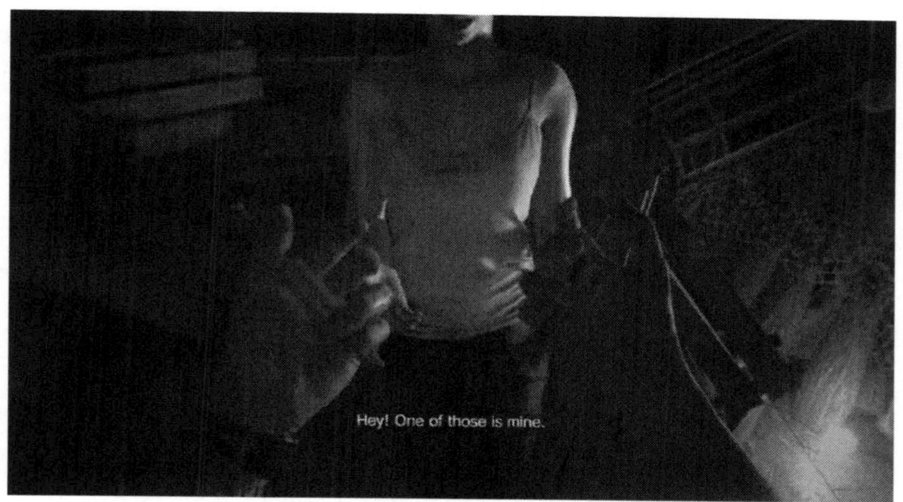

Zoe made 2 serums (2)

Fighting Jack again

Fighting Jack again (2)

Using one serum, Jack was finished

Jack was finished (2)

Now, there was only one Serum left.

The hard choice for Ethan was curing Mia or Zoe?

Now, there was only one Serum left. Ethan had to choose to cure either Zoe or Mia.

In this situation, what will your choice be?

Of course, I will choose to heal Mia, my wife. Zoe is a stranger after all :(

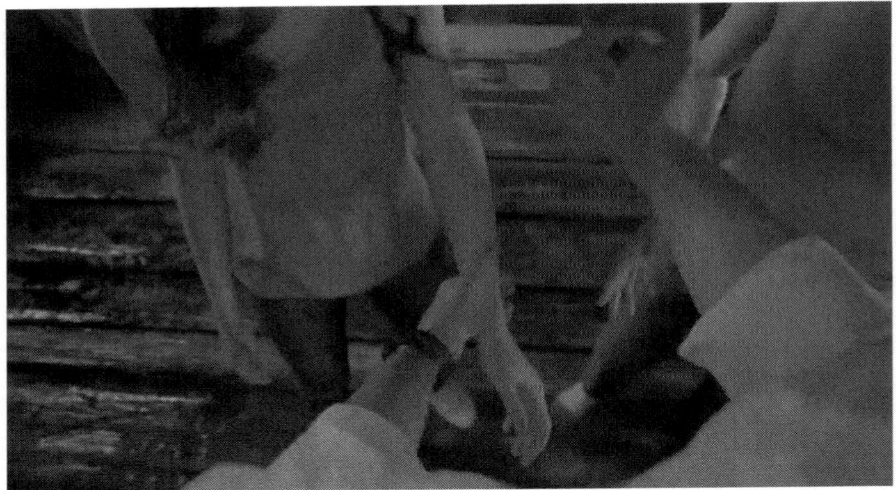

It was a hard choice.

Ethan chose to heal Mia.

Bitterly, Ethan chose Mia despite the favor owed to Zoe, and upset, she shouted at them to leave now. Ethan promised to send help but she spat the sentiments back at him. Riding away, both Ethan and Mia felt a bit guilty about getting away without Zoe, but more than that, Ethan urged Mia to remember more about what's going on.

Feeling upset, Zoe urged them to escape.

Ethan promised to send help.

Ethan promised to send help (2)

Ethan promised to send help (3)

Both Ethan and Mia felt guilty about leaving without Zoe

Both Ethan and Mia felt guilty about leaving without Zoe (2)

Mia didn't remember anything happened

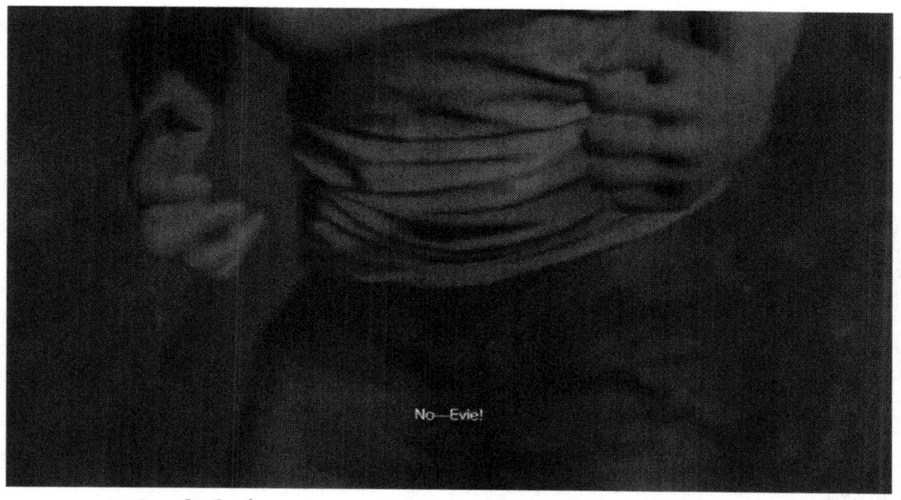

Mia didn't remember anything happened (2)